The World Is a Rainbow

The world is a rainbow
that's filled with many colors:
yellow, black and white and brown,
you see them all around.

The world is a rainbow
with many kinds of people.

It takes all kinds of people
to make the world go around.

Now you be you and I'll be me.
That's the way we were meant to be.

But the world is a mixing cup.
Just look what happens when you stir it up.

The world is a rainbow
with many kinds of people.

La La La La La La La

And when we work together,
it's such a sight to see.
The world is beautiful
when we live in harmony.

7

Now you be you and I'll be me.
That's the way we were meant to be.

But the world is a mixing cup.
Just look what happens when you stir it up.

The world is a rainbow
with many kinds of people.

And when we work together,
it's such a sight to see.

The world is beautiful
when we live in harmony.